The Monster

by

S. M. Tenneshaw

The Monster
by S. M. Tenneshaw

ISBN: 978-93-59328-00-3

Published by

DOUBLE 9 BOOKS

2/13-B, Ansari Road
Daryaganj, New Delhi – 110002
info@double9books.com
www.double9books.com
Tel. 011-40042856

ABOUT THE AUTHOR

S. M. Tenneshaw is an intriguing and brilliant author whose literary pursuits span a wide spectrum of genres, enthralling readers with stories that span science fiction, fantasy, mystery, and more. Despite having a modest public reputation, Tenneshaw's writing has a distinct and thought-provoking quality that leaves an indelible imprint on those who enter their literary worlds. Tenneshaw weaves intricate stories, develops complex characters, and creates immersive settings that take readers into richly conceived realms with a great command of storytelling. Their stories frequently explore significant subjects, stretching the imagination and questioning traditional viewpoints on life, mankind, and existence. Tenneshaw's work reflects a great love of literature as well as a desire to explore undiscovered realms of the human psyche and the cosmos. Their writing exemplifies the enduring fascination of storytelling, engaging both casual readers and dedicated fans seeking intellectually stimulating and emotionally relevant literary experiences. S. M. Tenneshaw's contributions continue to enhance the world of literature, allowing readers the opportunity to embark on literary excursions that both entertain and encourage thought long after the final page is turned in a literary environment that thrives on diversity and originality.

FRED TRENT pulled his coupe into the curb and leaned his head out the open window beside him.

"Hi, Joan, need any help?"

He called to a trim-looking girl in a nurse's uniform. Joan Drake was holding on to a leash with both hands, and her slender body was tugging against the leash as she strained against the pull of a Great Dane on the other end.

She looked over her shoulder as Trent called out, her blonde hair glinting in the warm afternoon sunlight. Blue eyes smiled an impish greeting at him.

"Hello, Fred. No thanks. Brutus and I get along famously."

Trent opened the car door and got out. He walked up the sidewalk and stood beside the girl.

"Business must be mighty slack for the great gland specialist, Stanley Fenwick. Is this all he can find for his pretty nurse to do?"

The girl sniffed. "Walking Brutus around has its compensations. At least he doesn't get fresh—like some people I know."

Fred grinned as he saw the huge dog suddenly turn on its leash and raise itself off the ground to stick out a long rapier-like tongue and lick the girl's cheek before she could move her head away.

"Down, Brutus! Down!" she called out, half-laughing.

Trent stepped in and pulled the big animal away from the girl, patting the dog's head as he did so.

"What was that you said about getting fresh?" Trent asked her. "Looks to me like the dog's life is the best around the Fenwick offices."

"Just don't get any ideas!" Joan Drake shot back.

"I've already got them," he replied. "Which reminds me, am I seeing you tonight?"

The girl held a tight grip on the leash and looked at him coyly.

"Let's see. We'll take in a movie, stop for a bite to eat at Joe's Hamburger Palace, and then drive out to North Butte. You'll park the car and then you'll ask me when I'm going to quit my job and settle down raising a family for you, and I'll say—"

"You'll say not until I get the biggest scoop in Arizona, a big raise, and a bonus as a down payment on a house," he completed her sentence.

"There! You see? We might just as well not have our date. In effect, we've had it already."

He looked at her for a long moment, and when he spoke again his voice had lost its humorous note.

"You forgot one very important item. When I ask you that usual question, and after you give your usual answer, I'll take you in my arms and tell you how much you mean to me, and—"

"You win," she interrupted him. "I had forgotten about that."

THE dog started to pull against the leash again and Fred reached out to help her hold the big animal in check. Then she looked at him again.

"What brings you to the outskirts of Tucson? Don't tell me there's a big story breaking on the edge of town."

He shook his head. "Not exactly. I'm on my way to the Rocket Research Proving Grounds. Just a routine story on the experiment they're going to pull off this evening. I've got to interview Mathieson, Gaddon, and a few other scientists on the project."

The girl laughed. "That's something of a coincidence. Dr. Blair Gaddon is in Dr. Fenwick's office right now."

Fred Trent's eyebrows raised in surprise.

"That so? Something wrong with him?"

"No. He's just having a physical checkup. Seems to be worried about his heart. Dr. Fenwick didn't need me since it's a routine job, so I took Brutus for a walk."

Trent nodded. "That's a bit of luck. I think I'll stick around and give Gaddon a lift out to the Proving Grounds. I wanted to talk to him anyway."

"In that case," the girl replied, "you can give me a hand putting Brutus back in his kennel. Once he gets out he's something of a problem."

Fred nodded, taking the leash from her hands and feeling the big dog tug against him.

"Never could figure out why Fenwick wanted a big hound like this. Seems to me a terrier would be more practical."

"That's a matter of taste," Joan answered. "Dr. Fenwick is very fond of Brutus—and so am I for that matter. But tell me something about this experiment you're covering."

They had turned in at a large Spanish type house that Trent knew served as a combination living quarters and office for the famous gland specialist. He shrugged.

"Don't know much about it myself. They're shooting off this new type rocket, a really big affair, loaded with all sorts of instruments. Some sort of experiment with cosmic rays. The rocket will go up to the outer layers of the Earth's atmosphere, where a clocked mechanism will release a parachute-attached section containing the instruments. This will float back to the surface of the Earth.

"There is one interesting thing about it though. They're also including a live animal with the instruments. A cat I believe. They want to see what effect the cosmic rays will have on a living creature."

The girl turned a shocked face toward him as they walked up the steps to the front door of the house. Trent could see a panel in the center of the door that opened from the inside, and over it, the sign, *Doctor is in, please ring*.

"But I think that's positively cruel!" Joan Drake said earnestly. "Subjecting an innocent animal to what may be certain death!"

Fred laughed at her concern. "Hold on, now. You should be the last one to take such an attitude. Doesn't medical science experiment on animals to find out about human ailments?"

"That's different," the girl insisted, opening the door and leading the way into a long hall. "Doctors know what they are doing—but this is a sheer waste of life ..."

TRENT let the dog pull him down the hall toward a door at the end which he knew opened on the backyard where the Great Dane was kept.

"Seems to me it's much the same thing," he answered her. "Scientists want to explore the mysteries of space, and the only way to do it is with an animal. Or would you like to make the trip—maybe I can arrange it? Would make a big story, just the one I've been waiting for."

"I believe you would at that!" she mocked, opening the rear door. "Here, give me the leash."

Trent handed over the leash to her and watched as she released the huge dog. Brutus flicked out a long tongue once again and caught the girl's cheek in a wet caress before she straightened.

"Brutus! Now get along with you!"

The dog took a leisurely bound through the door and into the backyard. Trent glanced through the door at the tall fenced-in yard with the large kennel that might well have served as a small garage. He stood beside the girl watching the big animal romp for a few moments, then she shut the door and they turned back down the hall.

"I'll have to go inside now, Fred," she said. "If you want to wait for Gaddon, have a seat. It shouldn't be long."

She started to turn in at a door marked private, when Fred pulled her gently around and before she could stop him, had kissed her.

"I was getting mighty jealous of Brutus. Now I feel better."

"I don't know which of you I prefer," she shot back, then smiled and pulled away from him.

He watched her open the office door and close it after her.

HE HAD lit his second cigarette and gotten halfway through his third magazine on the rack beside the chair when the office door opened again. He heard the pleasant voice of Dr. Stanley Fenwick.

"If every man had a heart as strong as yours, Blair, we wouldn't need half the doctors we have."

Then he heard the deep, gruff voice of Dr. Blair Gaddon half laugh.

"Thanks a lot, Fenwick. You've taken a load off my mind. Goodbye, Miss Drake."

He heard Joan reply and then saw Dr. Fenwick usher the physicist out into the hall.

Trent rose as the two men approached.

"Why, hello, Trent," Dr. Fenwick said.

Trent nodded at the tall, white-coated figure of the famous gland specialist.

"Afternoon, doctor."

Fenwick smiled at him. "Don't tell me you're waiting to see me?"

Fred shook his head. "Not exactly. I was waiting to see Dr. Gaddon though. I was on my way out to the Proving Grounds and I happened to stop by and talk to Miss Drake." He turned to the physicist, a bulky man with firm, hard features, who moved his large body with an almost cat-like grace.

"I hope you don't mind, Dr. Gaddon. Possibly I can give you a lift back out to the Base. I'm covering the launching for my paper."

Gaddon smiled at him. "But of course I don't mind. And I'll take you up on that offer. It'll save me a trip back to town to take one of the staff cars."

THE words had a friendly note to them, as did the smile on Gaddon's face. And yet, somehow, Fred Trent found that he did not like this man. It was nothing he could put his finger on, nothing he could rationalize, unless it was the coldly calculating look in the scientist's eyes.

"That's fine, doctor," Trent replied. "Shall we go?"

He turned and said good-bye to Fenwick and passed a smiling glance at the girl. He could see her blush slightly as Fenwick caught the glance and laughed. Then they were out of the house and Trent led the way to his car.

Inside, he started the motor and drove away. Beside him, Gaddon lit a cigar and blew a long plume of smoke through the open window.

"You said you wanted to talk to me, Trent?"

Fred nodded. "That's right, doctor. I'm writing up the rocket experiment for my paper, and I thought maybe you could give me a few details of interest." He paused for a moment, then asked: "Would it be too personal to ask if your visit to Dr. Fenwick had anything to do with the coming experiment?"

Gaddon shot a quick glance at him.

"Why do you ask that?"

Fred Trent shrugged. "It was just a thought. I heard Dr. Fenwick talking about your heart, but you look pretty healthy to me, so I thought maybe it was because Fenwick is a gland specialist and you might be talking to him about examining the cat after the rocket returns ..."

Gaddon laughed roughly. "A mighty clever reasoning, Trent, but not quite correct. The fact is, I was seeing the doctor for personal reasons. Just a physical checkup. It had nothing to do with the rocket experiment or the effect of the cosmic rays on the animal we're including in the experiment."

"It was just a thought, doctor," Trent replied, as he moved the coupe out on the open highway away from Tucson and toward the Rocket Proving Grounds on the desert flats in the distance.

"So now that we've disposed of that, what else would you like to know?" Gaddon asked him, a peculiar edge to his voice that Trent did not miss.

"Well, I would like to get a first hand bit of information on just exactly what you plan to prove with this experiment. If I'm correct, Dr. Mathieson, the head of the project, contends that cosmic rays may be lethal, and this experiment is to prove his point."

The physicist snorted. "It is no secret that Mathieson and myself disagree violently on that subject."

Trent's eyebrows raised. "Is that so? I wasn't aware of it?"

Gaddon paused, seeing that his words had slipped out too freely. Finally he said, "What I meant to say, Trent, is that up until now it has not been a public issue of disagreement. And I would prefer to have it remain a private matter until after the experiment."

"I see," Trent mused. "You have my word that I won't print anything you say without your permission. But just what is the difference of opinion between you and Mathieson?"

Gaddon took a long pull at his cigar and waited a few moments before replying. It was apparent to Trent that he was debating continuing the subject with a newspaperman. But Trent had gauged the man correctly. There was a flair of vanity in Gaddon that dated back to his English ancestry. Trent remembered that Gaddon, quite a figure in English scientific circles, had created a stir when he had come over to the United States to assist in rocket research at the Arizona proving grounds. It seemed that Gaddon had not wanted to take a back seat to the famed American scientist, Mathieson. It had made a few gossip columns in the newspapers before Washington put an official clamp on the matter.

NOW, as Trent waited for the Englishman to reply, he could almost sense the thoughts that were going through Gaddon's mind. The Englishman was debating whether to take an open stand against the viewpoints of his American colleague. But Trent felt that the British stubbornness in the man would make him reveal his own theories. Especially since Trent had already promised not to print anything without Gaddon's permission. That would give him an opportunity to gloat safely, should his own ideas be proven correct.

"Very well, Trent, I'll take you at your professional word to keep this matter confidential. But if what I contend is correct, you'll have a big story to tell."

Trent waited expectantly, not wanting to break the Englishman's train of thought.

"The fact is, Trent, that Mathieson is all wrong. To go even further, most of your American scientists don't have the haziest idea of exactly what the cosmic rays are. We in Britain have made quite exhaustive studies of the phenomena."

Trent didn't bother to argue with him. He only nodded his head. It would have been silly, he knew, to contradict Gaddon, to tell him that the English didn't know a thing more about the cosmic rays than the American scientists, that American science had made, and was continually making, exhaustive research into that scientific field of study on as great if not more so a scale than Britain could possibly achieve. It was only Gaddon's vanity talking, Trent knew, so he let him put in the barb of ridicule, waiting.

"I was sent over here, as you may know, to aid in the current experiment. To formulate it as a matter of fact. This test is being conducted to determine just what effect cosmic rays will have on a living organism. As I said, Mathieson, and your other scientists are of the opinion that the rays are lethal. That they will destroy life. In effect, that they are death rays.

"But I contend that they are wrong. What would you say if I told you that cosmic rays are the very source of life and energy in the universe?"

Trent whistled judiciously, and noted that Gaddon's face smiled at the apparent surprise Trent evinced.

"You find that a startling statement?"

Trent nodded. "I'd say that it sounded like the beginning of a very interesting theory."

"And you would be right," Gaddon replied, warming to his subject. "It is my contention that the cosmic rays will prove to be the fountain of youth that men have sought through the ages. That they will react on the glands of a living creature and produce immortality.

"Now take your choice. Whose theory would you rather believe? Mathieson's idiotic claims of a death ray, or mine as a source of the utmost benefit to science?"

Trent took a moment before replying. When he did so, he spoke with tact, and also with the feeling that his trip to Fenwick's office had proven very valuable. For there was a story here. A big story.

"I'd say, doctor, that I'd like to believe your theory was correct. But isn't it a little premature to be so definite about it?"

Gaddon snorted. "No more premature than Mathieson's. And I'll tell you something else, Trent. You may not realize it, but you're about to take part in what may be the biggest story of the century. And when it breaks, you'll remember our conversation here. I intend to prove that your American scientists are wrong."

Trent noticed the personal emphasis that Gaddon put in his last statement, but he was drawn away from the conversation as he turned the coupe into the guarded entrance to the proving grounds.

There was a moment of credential flashing to the guards, and a respectful salute to the scientist in the car beside Trent. Then Trent moved his coupe through the entrance and up the cement roadway to the Administration building.

As Gaddon got out of the car he turned to Trent.

"I'll leave you here. The members of the Press will be conducted to the launching site at dusk. I'll see you then. In the meantime, don't forget that you've given your word not to release any of the information I've given you."

Trent nodded and watched him walk away. He followed the Englishman with his eyes, a frown crossing his face. There was something too cocksure about the man. His ridicule of American scientists could be ignored, but the way he spoke about his theory, as if it had already been a proven fact against the ideas of Mathieson....

A faint chill ran up Fred Trent's back. He couldn't explain it. But it was there. An ominous note of foreboding.

He shrugged it off and left his car to walk toward the Administration building.

THE remaining hours of the afternoon dragged by in a monotony of idle speculation. Trent listened to the gathered newspapermen discussing the coming experiment at dusk, accompanied them as Dr. Mathieson, the head of the project, conducted them on a tour of the project, to the launching site, and then back to the central building.

The launching site itself had been an impressive sight. The huge rockets, much in appearance like the famed V2 of World War II, but on a much larger scale, were cradled in their launching platforms like some huge monsters about to be unleashed into the unsuspecting heavens.

They had listened as Mathieson explained the various number of instruments that were being included in the first rocket, to record its hurtling trip through the atmosphere to the outermost layers of the Earth's surface.

And they had been told of the other, and to the gathered newspapermen, the most interesting part, the inclusion of a cat in the rocket, in a large oxygen-fed chamber, to study the effects of the cosmic rays on a living creature.

Then back to the central building. Back to wait. And the tension began to mount. For the shadows were lengthening, the sun sinking behind the horizon to the west. The moment was now close at hand.

ASTOCKY figure detached itself from the shadows beside the huge bulk of the laboratory building and slowly edged out into the dusk.

It paused momentarily, to survey the scene. Sharp eyes scanned the looming rockets and their launching platforms, watchful, alert. They finally settled upon the armed guard who walked a measured distance back and forth in front of the rockets. Then the figure moved forward again, cautiously, purposefully.

The distance from the giant rockets shortened gradually, and then the guard, turning to retrace his steps, saw the approaching figure.

There was a snapping sound as a rifle was brought into position, and a rapping command barked out.

"Halt! Who goes there?"

The shadowy figure halted abruptly a short distance away from the guard. And a voice answered.

"Dr. Blair Gaddon."

The guard's rifle snapped into present arms and then back to the soldier's right shoulder.

"Oh, it's you, sir. Is there anything wrong? The launching is set for fifteen minutes from now, isn't it?"

Gaddon walked slowly up to the soldier and the guard could then see his face in the thickening shadows.

"That's right," Gaddon replied. "I'm making a last minute inspection."

The guard nodded. "Dr. Mathieson and the newspapermen will be along any minute, sir?"

Gaddon moved closer to the soldier, and then suddenly his hand came out of his coat pocket and there was a gun in it.

"Drop your rifle, soldier. Quick!"

The guard stared at the scientist in shocked astonishment.

"What is this, sir? A gag?"

Gaddon motioned with his gun.

"It is no gag! Do as I say—or must I shoot?"

THERE was an ominous note in Gaddon's voice. And a strained quality to it that told the guard the man meant what he said. Very slowly the soldier removed the rifle from his shoulder and dropped it to the ground.

Gaddon motioned with his gun.

"Now step back! Move!"

The guard moved slowly back a pace, and then the Englishman stepped forward and kicked the rifle away from the man. Then he motioned around the rocket.

"Now move over around the side of the number one rocket to the far side of number two."

He watched as the guard turned and began to walk slowly around the huge base of the waiting rocket. He followed the soldier.

"I don't know what this is all about, Dr. Gaddon," the guard protested. "But I can tell you one thing, you're playing with the United States Government right now. When Dr. Mathieson hears about this—"

"When Dr. Mathieson hears about this, soldier, I'll be a long way from here—out at the edge of space itself!"

Gaddon could hear the guard draw in his breath sharply, but the man kept walking around to the far side of the second rocket cradle.

"You can't mean that you're going to go up—"

The soldier's voice broke off uncertainly and Gaddon laughed shortly.

"You are a discerning man, soldier. That is exactly what I intend to do. And I warn you, don't make a false move or I'll shoot. My plans are made and I intend to carry them out!"

They had reached the far side of the second rocket now, away from view of the rest of the buildings, out of sight. Away in the distance the faint outlines of the great wire fence circling the testing grounds could be seen, and beyond that, the twinkling lights of Tucson, already visible in the dusk.

"This is far enough," Gaddon said suddenly.

He watched as the soldier halted. Then Gaddon moved up quickly behind the man. Before the soldier sensed what was about to occur, Gaddon's hand raised over his head and the butt of the weapon in his hand crashed against the back of the man's head.

There was a soft groan in the shadows as the soldier crumpled limply to the ground. In the silence that followed, Gaddon's tense breathing was the only sound. He looked down at the still body of the unconscious man, then he quickly turned and retraced his footsteps back the way he had come.

When he had reached the far side of the first rocket, he stopped before the metal steps of the cradle leading up to the closed door of the rocket. He looked quickly about him, making sure that nobody was in close proximity, then he threw his gun under the rocket beside the rifle of the soldier, and ran up the steps.

A cool breeze sprang up in the western night and whispered softly around Gaddon as he fumbled for a moment with a switch set in the smooth side of the rocket beside the sealed door.

There was a click, finally, and the door slid open.

Gaddon took a last look about him and then quietly slipped through the opening. A moment later there was the sound of the door sliding shut.

Inside the rocket, Gaddon lit a small pocket flash and looked around him. A soft sound struck his ears. The mewing sound of a cat. He turned the flash on the startled animal and a low laughter crept from his throat.

He moved through the large instrument chamber then and sat on the floor beside the cat.

Then the flash went out and his laughter came again ...

"ALL right, gentlemen, the time has come. In a few minutes an automatic control, synchronized with controls in the rocket will be set off in the main laboratory building. If we want to watch the launching we'll have to hurry."

Fred Trent listened to the voice of Mathieson, and saw the famed American scientist start out of the central lobby toward the launching site. The gathered newspapermen followed, their voices filled with excitement now that the moment had come.

Trent followed along with them, but felt a peculiar tenseness within him. He had been watching for Gaddon to make his appearance. But as yet the Englishman had not showed up. Was it possible that he wasn't going to watch the rocket launching? As Trent followed the others out into the gathering night, he frowned to himself. It was certainly strange. And entirely unlike the blustering manner Gaddon had displayed on the drive back from Tucson. Or had the man suddenly realized that he had made a fool of himself and was taking this easy way out?

But that too didn't seem natural. And Trent found himself edging forward through the ranks of the newsmen, until he had reached the side of Mathieson.

The scientist was talking to one of the journalists as they rounded the corner of the Administration building. Now the rockets were in sight, standing tall and immense in the shadows.

Mathieson held his hand up in a gesture of halt, and the men behind him drew into a compact circle.

Fred turned to Mathieson.

"Dr. Mathieson, isn't Dr. Gaddon going to be here for the launching?"

The head of the rocket project turned to Trent. Fred could see a suddenly puzzled look in his eyes.

"Yes, that is strange ..." Then he laughed. "I suppose Gaddon is in the laboratory supervising the firing controls. Well, if he wants to miss the show, that's his fault. He knows the schedule."

Trent accepted the scientist's words without replying. But he still wasn't satisfied. What was it that Gaddon had said in the car about the biggest story of the year? What had the man meant? Question after question arose in Trent's mind as he stood there, and always the queer feeling inside him grew in intensity. He could not place his finger on it, but somehow, he knew that something was wrong.

But then his suspicions were put aside for the moment as he heard Mathieson say:

"All right, gentlemen, the time is nearly here. In precisely one minute the rocket will be fired."

The statement was made with a quiet eagerness, and then suddenly the gathered witnesses grew silent.

Trent's eyes, along with the others, fastened on the looming bulk of the waiting rocket.

And the seconds ticked off in Fred's mind.

As he counted them, he thought that it seemed impossible that within a very few moments that gigantic hulk of smooth, tapered metal would dislodge itself from the cradle it rested in with a burst of roaring flame. That in another few seconds it would shoot into the blackened sky, and in a few short minutes would reach unbelievable heights in the heavens, to the edge of space itself before the automatic controls released the instrument section to be returned safely to earth.

And the seconds passed.

"Time!"

Trent heard the voice of Mathieson rap the word out sharply.

And then there was a roar of sound from the cradled rocket.

A spear of flame shot from its base, exploding the night into a brilliant display of pyrotechnics.

THE roaring grew louder as the tremendous power of the now unleashed rockets took hold of the night air. Fred watched as the flames grew white-hot bright, and then he saw the gigantic rocket shudder in its cradle.

The shudder grew into a spasm of movement, and then slowly, but steadily growing faster, the rocket lifted from its cradle.

Fred's eyes were fastened on the rocket now, a feeling of awe sweeping through him. He suddenly realized how puny man was against the forces man could unleash. Forces that here were being utilized to scientific ends, but forces that upon a moment's notice, could in turn be unleashed upon the rest of humanity in a burning, devastating terror of death.

And as the thought flitted across his mind, he saw the rocket gather speed as it left its cradle. It was now rising in a swift, sure arc, lashing into the dark sky like a fury.

And then the terrible speed of the rocket took hold against the forces of gravity and it shot into the heavens, its roaring becoming a fading hiss of sound, the brilliant flash of flame from its exploding tubes, a receding beacon of light that gradually faded to a pinpoint far over their heads.

After the terrific thunder of sound that had accompanied the launching of the rocket, the sudden silence now was almost palpable. The gathered witnesses stood mutely, awe still in their eyes, their ears still ringing with the sound of the takeoff.

Finally the voice of Mathieson broke the quiet night air.

"Well, gentlemen, that's it. Tomorrow morning we'll scout the returned section. It should land somewhere in the open country to the south. We've computed that pretty carefully. I guess that's about all for—"

His voice broke off suddenly and Fred Trent heard what must have distracted the scientist.

A man was shouting from the vicinity of the second rocket, and as they looked, a dim figure could be seen staggering away from the side of the other rocket, coming slowly toward them.

"Good Lord!" Mathieson breathed. "What's that man doing out there? He could have been killed!"

Then suddenly they saw the staggering figure stumble on the ground.

And then Trent and the others were racing across the ground to the side of the fallen man.

When they reached him, Mathieson came forward and knelt beside the figure.

"Why, it's one of the guards!" he said in shocked surprise.

And it was then that the strange feeling of foreboding hit Fred again. As he knelt beside the groaning guard, it swept over him in a chilling wave. He lifted the man's head from the ground and the guard opened his eyes. He recognized the face of Mathieson as the scientist looked anxiously in his direction.

"Good heavens, man, what happened? You were ordered to leave five minutes before launching time!"

The guard's mouth opened as he struggled to a sitting position. The man's hand reached up and touched the back of his head painfully.

"Sir—Gaddon—Dr. Gaddon attacked me ..."

There was a momentary stunned silence as the soldier's words sunk in on the gathered men.

"*What?*" Mathieson's voice was incredulous.

And as Trent watched the soldier nod his head, the suspicion he had felt suddenly overwhelmed him in a grim realization. Even as the soldier blurted out pain-filled words, Trent knew somehow what he was going to say.

"Gaddon—he pulled a gun on me ... He forced me to the far side of number two—he said he was going up in the rocket—he said he had plans—then he hit me with the gun ... I came to when the rocket went off—I was away from the blasts, luckily ..."

Then the soldier was standing on his feet again, swaying as he fought to clear his fogged senses.

But Trent was no longer aware of the soldier. And he saw that Mathieson was no longer looking at the guard. For a brief instant their eyes met, and Trent saw a stunned look in the scientist's, then Fred's gaze swept up into the night. Up into the darkened sky where, miles above them, the hurtling rocket was even now reaching the apex of its flight.

Up where a man rode on a perilous trip into the unknown.

GADDON hunched in the darkness of the rocket, waiting. He had counted the remaining minutes off, one by one. And he knew that finally the moment was at hand.

It would be too late now to stop him. They had not noticed his absence, and if they had, they would not delay the launching for him. He had taken that fact into consideration.

And now that the moment was close to completion, he felt a glowing sense of triumph within him. He would now show those fools, and especially Mathieson. He would prove conclusively that cosmic rays were what he had said they were—a source of the energy of life, a fountain from which youth and vitality would pour, making his body immortal. He would go down in history as one of the greats of science. A man who had risked his life to prove his theory. A man who would be the first to achieve the goal of the ages, the dream of the philosophers, eternal life.

The triumph would be his. *All* his!

And the rocket tubes exploded into sound.

Gaddon tensed in the darkness, gripping the safety straps he had attached to himself. Beside him he felt the cat let out a frightened mewing sound as the roar of the exploding rocket power grew. He felt the furry body rubbing against his side, seeking sanctuary against this dread sound.

And then the rocket trembled with sudden movement.

It was slow at first, but then it grew faster, and Gaddon felt a faint intensity of fear in his temples at the shuddering power of that movement.

And then he felt the blood draining from his head, making him faint with dizziness as the rocket accelerated suddenly into a terrible burst of speed.

He could feel it moving swiftly through the atmosphere now, feel the tortured rush of air that whipped against the sides of the projectile in a moaning dirge that mingled with the roar of the exploding rocket fuel.

And as the seconds passed, he became accustomed somewhat to the increasing velocity of the projectile, and the dizziness passed from his head. Then he became aware of the trembling body of the cat beside him and a soft laughter rose in his throat.

But it died stillborn as the roar of the rockets grew to a thundering hiss now in his ears.

And he felt the cool sweetness of the automatically released oxygen fill the chamber about him and he drank it into his lungs hungrily.

With each second now, he knew the projectile was racing higher into the rarefied atmosphere, heading steadily out to where the air of earth would be almost non-existent.

And a grim smile crossed his face in the darkness, for he knew that shortly the rocket would enter the outermost layers and the cosmic rays would play with all their energies upon the projectile.

And he tensed suddenly.

There was a glow that sprang into being in the chamber about him.

It was dim at first. But it grew steadily in intensity around him, revealing the interior of the chamber in its weird light.

An exultation swept through him then. He knew they had entered the field of the cosmic rays, and that the manifestation of light he saw was a result of those forces of nature.

Beside him the cat mewed plaintively in fear and huddled closer against Gaddon's body. His eyes watched the tiny creature for a moment and then swept around the large chamber at the massed instrument panels that were recording every minute fraction of a second of the flight.

And the glow grew.

And suddenly the hissing of the exploding rocket fuel began to diminish in volume. The apex of the flight was nearly at hand then.

And the glow around Gaddon began to color. From a weird phosphorescent whiteness it changed to a dull but intense yellow. And with the change, a strange feeling crept through his body.

IT TUGGED at him with invisible hands. It played upon his every nerve, his every fiber, the innermost feelings of his sensibility. It grew stronger, this alien probing within him, grew as the glow pulsed in the chamber around him.

And suddenly, instead of a fierce feeling of triumph, a sense of dread swept through him. He fought at the gripping sensations within him, tried to dispel them, to no avail. They grew stronger, like invisible hands that were changing the very essence of life inside him.

And as the thought passed through his suddenly tortured mind, he realized that was exactly what was taking place. A change. A change beyond his comprehension, beyond the understanding of any man. Beyond—

And the whining fearful mew of the cat beside him changed. It tensed against his body, and the whine in its animal throat became an irate hiss. He looked down and saw the hackles rising on the back of the cat, saw the creature looking up at him now, not with wide frightened eyes of appeal, but with a ferocity of wildness that brought a chill to his inner being.

And the glow grew around him, brilliant yellow in texture now. And with the increasing brilliance of the light, the feeling of change grew within him.

It was stronger than he now. It held his every heartbeat in its pulsing grip. It throbbed in his temples, ached to the ends of his toes, set his body aflame with it.

And the cat suddenly lunged against him, its sharpened claws biting through his garments and into his flesh.

His hands reached down in a quick movement and gripped the body of the cat. He tore the raking claws away from his body and held the cat in the air beside him.

The creature writhed in his grasp, fighting madly to escape. And as his grip tightened on the animal, the eyes of the cat suddenly locked with his.

He felt the forces within him reach a crescendo at that moment. And his body was frozen immobile, his eyes locked on the cat's eyes, burning into the animal, the animal burning into him. Burning and burning ...

It could only have been a matter of seconds, he knew. But they were seconds that stretched into the farthermost reaches of eternity. Seconds that lived a million years and passed in another fleeting instant.

And then he could move again.

And he felt strange as he moved. It was as if he was another person, as if the body he moved was alien to him, as if it had never belonged to him, to any man, to any thing.

And his eyes tore away from the now dulled expression in the cat's eyes. He did not find it strange that this was so. He knew in some inner sense that the mighty life force in him had quelled the cat. Had stilled the fighting in its feline eyes.

And he saw his hands clutching the body of the cat.

He stared at them for a long disbelieving moment. For they were not the hands he had known. They were not the hands of Blair Gaddon. They were not the hands of any man. They were long and tapered and claw-like. There was dark fuzzy fur around them, fur that was cat-like.

Deep within him a fear struggled upward through his mind. A cold dread that forced his lips to move, to utter a gasp of the terror he felt.

And the sound left his lips.

It left his lips and echoed terribly in his ears. A harsh sound. A mewing sound. *A cat sound ...*

The creature in his grasp struggled feebly then. It was a small movement, a movement without vitality, almost without life. And as the creature moved, a sense of rage welled up inside him. A rage that he could not control, an anger that he wanted to unleash to its fullest. And as it took possession of him, the human part of his mind shrieked and forced words from his lips.

"You fiend! You fiend of hell!"

And his fingers crept up to the neck of the cat and closed in a mighty grip. He felt the animal give a single desperate effort in his grasp, but his grip tightened and he saw the mouth of the creature open wide and heard a faint hissing gasp as its tongue stuck far out and its eyes bulged in a last moment of life.

Then the animal lay limp in his claw-like hands and he dropped it to the floor of the rocket chamber, a growl of frustration leaving his lips.

He stared at the cat's body for a moment, then his fingers stole up and touched his face. He felt the hairy coarseness of it, the furry tingle of his once smooth skin. And he screamed into the now fading glow that he knew was the energy of the cosmic rays.

"No! No! It can't be true! I haven't *changed* like this! I—I—*meowrr* ..."

Around him the thunder of the rocket fuel suddenly vanished into silence, and then the rocket gave a lurch.

Deep within his mind he knew that the instrument section had been released from the main body of the projectile, and even now he knew the sealed chamber was falling back toward the earth, back toward the atmosphere where the parachute would take hold and drift the chamber safely down to the Arizona soil.

And a dread closed over him in that moment. Back to the men. Back to the things of men. Back he must go, a mewing thing that was not a man. A thing that he felt was taking hold of him, driving the last vestige of human instinct from him.

He fought it. He fought it mewing on the floor of the rocket chamber.

"HE MUST have gone mad!"

Fred Trent pulled his gaze from the sky and looked with stunned eyes at the figure of Dr. Mathieson standing beside him. The scientist was trembling with an inner feeling, and his head was shaking in disbelief.

"Gaddon! The man is going to his death! It's insane!"

Again Mathieson's voice broke the silence in the huddled group of men. Then the newspapermen came to life and excited talk became a jabber of words around them. Trent took the arm of Mathieson and turned him. He tried to lead the scientist away from the newspapermen but one of them stepped forward and grabbed his arm.

"But why did he do it, doctor? The man must have had a reason!"

Mathieson shook his head numbly.

"I—I don't know, unless ..." his voice trailed off for a moment and then he spoke again. "Unless he really believed what he said ..."

"What did he say, doctor?" the newsman asked.

There was a puzzled note to Mathieson's voice as he answered.

"He disagreed with me on the supposed effects of the cosmic rays. It has been my contention that they are of lethal effect, and Gaddon maintained that I was wrong. He kept insisting that they were a source of life energy. That was why we decided to experiment with an animal—to see what effect the rays would have on a living creature ...

"But this! I never dreamed of such a possibility—to prove his point he signed his own death warrant!"

"That's a story, doctor, a real story!"

Trent heard the newsman exclaim excitedly. And then it came to him that the real story was as yet untold. The real story that had been unfolded in his car earlier that day.

Fred moved suddenly away from the clamor of the newsmen around the scientist. He knew what he had to do.

He hurried across the ground to his waiting coupe outside the Administration building. Then he got behind the wheel and started the motor.

He drove to the gate and waited until the guard passed him through, then he turned up the road toward Tucson.

As he drove he felt an odd tenseness sweep through him. For he was thinking of what Gaddon had said on the drive up to the Proving Grounds. He was remembering the man's words on the cosmic rays and the secret of eternal life they held. And Fred Trent knew that this was the biggest story. The story that he alone held. It was the big break that he had been waiting for. It would be his exclusive. The inside, personal story of a man who had died to prove his theory. Told as Gaddon himself had related it. With all the vanity of the man, all the pompous assurance he had shown. It would make the headlines and feature sections all over the country. The story of a man who had flown to his death in quest of immortality.

And then Trent's thoughts grew sober suddenly. But was he going to his death? Could he be sure that Mathieson was right? That Gaddon was suffering from some streak of insanity that had manifested itself in this final venture of madness? Or could it be that Gaddon might be right, that ...

Trent set his lips and sighed. No, that couldn't be true. It was beyond the comprehension of man.

What mattered now was the story. The story that would put his name in a thousand papers all over the country. And he thought in that moment of Joan Drake. A warm smile pulled at his lips as he thought of her. This would force her to quit her job now and marry him. The one condition she had made—he had finally overcome.

He thought of the date he was supposed to have with her that evening. It would have to be postponed until later. The story came first. And then ...

He drove his car swiftly through the outskirts of the city and into the main part of town. Then he pulled up before the offices of the *Tucson Star* and left his car at the curb.

HE ENTERED the building, took the elevator to his floor and walked into the city room. The clatter of typewriters met his ears and the sound was sweet to him in that moment.

He crossed swiftly to his desk and sat dawn. Then he motioned to a copy boy. The boy came up to his desk.

"Jerry, tell the chief to hold up the form on page one. I've got a special—an accident out at the Proving Grounds. Headline copy."

The youth hurried away toward the office of the City Editor, and Fred picked up his phone and dialed a number. He waited a moment and then the voice of Joan Drake came across the wire.

"Dr. Fenwick's office."

"Joan, this is Fred."

The girl's voice laughed across the wire. "Don't tell me you're planning to break our date? Just when I get all dressed up."

A smile crossed Trent's lips. "You're almost psychic, honey. Fact is, I was calling to tell you I'll be a little late."

There was a pause and when the girl spoke again there was an injured note in her voice.

"Well, that's a fine thing. I wait here deliberately after hours for you to pick me up and now you tell me you'll be late! Just what's so more important than me right now?"

"I haven't got time to tell you now, Joan, but believe me, I've got the break of the year. A story that will rock the front pages across the country. I'll tell you all about it later. You can wait at Fenwick's place. He won't mind, will he?"

He could hear the girl sniff on the other end of the wire.

"I don't suppose he will, but I don't think I can say the same for myself."

"That's a good girl," Trent laughed. "Just wait for me. It may be an hour or so—"

"An *hour* or so! What are you writing, the great American novel?"

He looked up and saw the frowning face of the City Editor approaching his desk. He spoke hurriedly.

"I've got to sign off now. The boss is coming up. I'll see you later. Give my regards to Brutus."

He replaced the phone as the editor reached his desk.

"What's all this about a remake on the front page, Trent?"

Fred nodded. "That's right, chief. The biggest story since the atom bomb. Listen!"

He gave a short account of what had happened, and then added the personal details of his talk with Gaddon. He saw the eyes of the editor widen as he went on, and by the time he had finished, there was a look of excitement on the editor's face.

"Get to that story, Trent. Write it hot, and write it fast. I'll hold the first form and tear down the front page. Stress the human interest angle. Play it up big. We'll hit the news wires with it after we go to press."

Then a smile crossed the editor's face. "And you'll get a by-line on this, Trent, that ought to put you in for some big money. Nice work."

Then he turned on his heel and was hurrying across the city room toward his glassed-in office, hollering for a copy boy as he went.

Trent turned back to his desk and slipped a sheet of paper into his typewriter. There was a tenseness around his eyes as he brought his fingers down on the keys. For a moment the old questions rose again in his mind. *Was Gaddon right? Could it be possible that ...*

Then he forgot everything but the story. And his fingers clicked against the keys, putting it down on paper.

THE rocket chamber swayed gently through the night air, whistling its way slowly downward, moving more slowly as the great parachute above it caught in the rapidly thickening density of the cabin's atmosphere.

Inside it, the thing that had been Gaddon, the thing that was no longer a man, sat on the floor of the chamber, idly toying with the dead body of the cat.

Strange thoughts coursed through the mind inside its head. Half of the mind that belonged to Gaddon, and half of the mind that was an alien thing, a creature unnamed.

There was a thought of killing and the thought was good. The claw-like hands played with the cat's dead body, fondling it idly, wishing it were still alive so that it might die again.

And the other part of its mind, the part that still knew it was Gaddon, rebelled against the thought. Tried to drive it away. Tried to move that alien intelligence into the rear of his consciousness.

A growl left his lips as he struggled with it. And then a whimpering sound.

For now the alien thought of killing and the joy it had experienced as the cat died scant moments before, was replaced by another thought. A thought of loneliness.

It was a weird feeling, an utter loneliness that came from the great void beyond man's planet. It cried out in silent protest for it knew it was alone in this world of men.

And it knew it would remain alone, friendless. For what manner of men such as the other part of its mind showed would react in a friendly fashion? Where would be their common meeting ground? There could only be one, it knew. And that one was fear. Fear and the hate that went with it.

A growl left its lips again, and Gaddon's thoughts tried to force their way through. Tried and failed again.

But was it necessary to want companionship? It thought about that for a moment. And then the alien beast thoughts grew sharper, clearer. It knew suddenly that it did not want man's compassion. It knew that there was only one driving thought in it. Hate. Hate that would inspire fear. Fear that would freeze its victim into terror. And terror that would be replaced by death. And then it would be happy again. Happy to sit and fondle the thing that had been alive. And it knew something else. It knew that a hunger would have to be satisfied. A hunger that called for flesh.

Deep, primeval thoughts raced through it then. Thoughts that were spawned in the ancient jungles of a new and steaming world. A world where great cats roamed, where screams of cat-rage split the air as tawny bodies arced in lightning leaps to land on the trembling bodies of their victims. It was a satisfying thought. A thought that spanned the ages of Earth, a sense that was inherent in all cat minds through the ages.

And as the thought raced through that portion of its mind, the part that was Gaddon struggled to fight it back. For it realized with a sickness that spread horror through it that the thought was part of the animal existence that had been created in him. Part of the monster that lay by instinct in all feline creatures. And Gaddon knew that the dead creature at his feet, the limp and twisted body of the cat, had died long before his hands had crushed it in their mighty grip. For the essence of that life, that animal existence, had been merged with him, fused by a mighty source from outer space.

AND as he struggled with the thought, fought to regain the balance of control of the strange body that was now his, the rocket chamber swayed in a gust of wind from without. And as he clutched the sides of the chamber with his strong claw-like hands, the chamber gave a bounding lurch as it struck the ground a glancing blow.

There was a grating sound as the metal chamber gouged into the earth, sank its weight upon the Arizona soil. And the thing was thrown violently against the side of the chamber.

Then there was quiet again.

Gaddon's mind fought to the fore, took control of that feline man-shape that was his, struggled to its feet and moved in a lithe bound to the opposite side of the chamber. A clawed hand reached up where Gaddon knew the release mechanism of the door lay, and pressed it.

The door slid back with a sliding sound and the cool night air rushed in upon it.

Gaddon moved his cat-body through the opening and bounded to the ground in a lithe, powerful movement. He felt new muscles react as he landed on the ground, and knew that there was a great strength in them. Strength that was waiting to be used.

And he felt the other thoughts starting to move forward in his mind again and he forced them back. He knew he must keep control of that mind. For there was something that he must do.

He thought desperately about it. And the pattern became clearer in his mind.

The cosmic rays. The reaction in his body. He had sought immortality in the door to outer space and had found a monster waiting for him. A force that had changed his glands, grown the shaggy fur on his body. Glands that had warped his mind. Opened an age-old cunning of feline thought.

Glands.

Gaddon's thoughts whipped the word. Held it. Knew it must be the answer. And then it found a prayer of hope. And a name that went with that thought.

"Fenwick! I've got to reach Fenwick before it's too late. *Before it's too late!*"

His voice came hoarsely, strangely formed. And he looked wildly about him. He saw, off in the distance, a glowing of lights in the night. And he knew somehow that it was the city of Tucson.

And in that city, at its very edge, was a house he must reach.

He stumbled away into the darkness, feeling his limbs move rapidly then, smoothly, covering the ground in great leaping strides.

And though Gaddon's thoughts kept the balance of control, deep inside his mind, the monster growled with a cunning laughter ...

FRED TRENT pulled the last sheet of paper from his typewriter and leaned back in his chair exhausted. That was it, the end of the story. He waved his hand at a copy boy and the boy ran up to take the final page. Each sheet had been taken like that, to be immediately set in the composing room. Now it was finished, the story of the year.

And as Trent slowly lit a cigarette and inhaled deeply, he knew that he had done a good job on the story. And a smile crossed his face as he thought of it. His future was assured now. There could be no more stopgaps, no more delays in his plans to marry Joan and settle down. And the girl would have to agree. For the first time in many months, Fred felt that his troubles were over with. And the feeling was nice. It spread through him and he was content.

He glanced at his wrist watch and frowned. The story had taken longer than he had anticipated. It was nearly eleven. Some of the enthusiasm ran out of him as he thought of Joan waiting for him at Fenwick's. He could imagine how angry she must be by now.

He got up quickly from his desk and reached for his hat. As he started to walk away, the phone on his desk rang.

He stepped back and picked up the receiver.

"Trent speaking."

"*Fred!*"

Trent heard his name uttered in terror across the wire and he felt a chill run through him as he recognized the voice. It was Joan Drake.

"Joan, what's wrong?" he asked anxiously.

"Fred! Come quickly! Bring help before it's too late—he'll kill us!"

"Joan! For God's sake, calm down! Now what's the matter?" His voice held a tenseness in it as he spoke.

"It's Gaddon, Fred! Only it isn't Gaddon—it's a monster! He'll kill us!"

"*Gaddon?*" Trent's voice spoke incredulously. "But that's imposs—"

"Oh, Fred, hurry— I—oh—no—no! Keep away—"

He heard the girl scream over the phone then. And he heard something else. A growling sound. A sound of animal noise unlike any other sound he had ever heard. And then as he shouted into the phone: "Joan! Joan!" the line went dead.

He stood for a moment, staring stupidly at the receiver in his hand. Then he slammed it back on its cradle and turned. He nearly knocked over the copy boy who hollered at him.

"Hey, Trent, the boss wants you in his office!"

But he swept by the boy unheeding. He didn't wait for the elevator. He took the stairs in leaping bounds, and then he was on the main floor of the building and out on the street.

He slammed the door of his car shut and started the motor. His hands trembled as he meshed the gears and shot the coupe away from the curb. Then he was moving swiftly through the traffic.

As he turned down the street where Fenwick's office was, Fred Trent's mind was a whirl of confused thought.

There was fear there. Fear and dread. And there was puzzlement too. A puzzlement that made his brain spin. Joan had spoken with terror in her voice. Terror that had said somebody was going to kill. And Joan was not a girl to be easily frightened. And she had mentioned Gaddon's name. Gaddon, the man who had shot into the heavens in an experimental rocket. Gaddon, who was supposed to be dead.

HE FELT now that same feeling that had crept through him after the launching. The feeling that had whispered in his mind that maybe Gaddon had been right after all. That maybe he wouldn't die. That maybe ... And now the dread swept him. For he thought of the sound he had heard over the phone. The last sound before the line went dead. The sound of an animal growling in wrath. And he remembered the girl's scream about a monster.

A cold sweat was on his forehead as he pulled the coupe into the curb in front of the Fenwick house. He switched off the motor and closed the car door after him.

Then he was hurrying up the walk to the front door, his eyes taking in the house in a swift glance, noting that the lights were lit in the consultation room. Lights that slivered out from the closed venetian blinds.

He stood then on the front porch, his hand closing over the knob of the door.

It was locked.

He pressed the bell then and heard its clarion sound inside the house. But other than that there was nothing to be heard. A deep, ominous silence that somehow brought a feeling of panic to him. Was he too late?

And then suddenly the panel in the front of the door opened and a face peered out at him.

Fred Trent felt the blood drain from his lips. A paralysis seemed to grip his body at what he saw framed in the opening.

For it was not the face of a human being. And yet, it was not the face of an animal. It was a horrible, twisted, cat-like visage that peered out at him, furred and ugly, with bared teeth and glowing, feline eyes.

And as he looked, a sound came from the twisted lips. It was the same sound he had heard over the telephone. The sound of a growling rage.

And as the sound hit his ears, a terrible realization swept over him. For his eyes, riveted on that monstrous countenance, had registered an impossible fact upon his mind.

As twisted as it was, as horribly changed into an animal grimace, it was the face of someone he knew—the English scientist, Blair Gaddon!

And then suddenly the face vanished from the opening. And Fred Trent felt his paralysis leave him. He knew now that he should never have come alone. That he should have called the police first. That he—

The door swung open then and Trent found himself facing the thing that had been Gaddon.

He took a backward step and started to turn and run for his car and help, but he was too slow.

An arm shot out and a claw-like hand suddenly gripped his shoulder in a swift, steel-like movement. He felt himself being pulled forward and into the house, as another growl snarled from the lips of the creature.

Trent tried to break the grip of that vise-like hand. He tried to smash his fist into the ugly visage of a face that confronted him. But he was like a child in that grip. And like a child, he was hurled across the hall, and he heard the door slam shut behind him.

As he got slowly to his feet and turned to face the creature, he heard a sobbing sound from the open door of the consultation room. It was the voice of Joan Drake.

And then the monster had reached him and the clawed hand reached out and spun him through the doorway, into the consultation room. And he heard a growling voice utter harshly: "You will regret this interference, Trent!"

And he knew that it was the voice of Blair Gaddon. And yet he also knew that it was not the same voice. It was changed. It had a bestial quality to it.

Then Trent looked around him. He saw Joan Drake, huddled in a corner of the room, beside Dr. Stanley Fenwick. The specialist was sitting in a chair, holding his right hand to his mouth. Fred could see blood oozing from a gash in the surgeon's lips.

AND then he heard another sound. A sound from without the house, coming from the rear. It was the baying of Brutus. The big dog must have sensed the presence of the monster. And it was protesting in its animal voice, a mournful dirge.

Then his attention was drawn once again to the animal body of Blair Gaddon. And now that the first shock had left him, Trent stared at the man. He heard the girl sob.

"Fred! I told you to bring help—"

"Be quiet!" the voice of Gaddon issued from the twisted lips. And the girl's sob stifled itself in a look of dread.

Then the face that had been Gaddon turned to Trent. There was a twisted leer to it, and Fred sensed that there was a struggle going on in that warped mind.

"You are Gaddon? The Blair Gaddon who went up with the experimental rocket?" Trent's voice came incredulously.

The face of the creature twisted in a grimace of acknowledgment.

"Yes, Trent. I am Blair Gaddon. I am not a pretty sight to look at, am I?" Words left the twisted lips, and there was a bestial pain in them.

"But—you're supposed to be dead! Mathieson—"

A strange sound of irony came from Gaddon.

"Mathieson was right about the cosmic rays—I know that now. Look at me! You see what has happened to me? I sought immortality through the life energy of space—and look at me!"

Horror reflected in Fred's eyes in that moment. For he felt the pained terror in the voice of the animal shape before him. And he saw the claw-like hands clench spasmodically.

"My glands!" the voice screamed. "The cosmic rays reacted on them— fed the essence of the cat into them—changed me into this monstrous being!"

Trent stared at the rage-filled face. Felt the emotion that was sweeping through the creature. Felt a sudden compassion that was erased by the bestial look that came into the monster's eyes.

And then it turned toward the chair where Fenwick sat. The doctor was looking at the creature, his eyes wide and terrified.

"But what do you expect me to do for you, Gaddon? Why do you stand here threatening—" Fenwick's voice came hoarsely.

"Why? You fool! Because there is so little time! I am changing! Even now my human instincts are nearly gone!... You're a gland specialist! There is something you can do—stop this change—stop it!"

Fenwick shook his head slowly. "You're raving like a madman, Gaddon. I'm not a God—do you think I can change something that is beyond human understanding? If you'll only let me call in the authorities ..."

A growl of rage left Gaddon's animal lips. "Authorities! So you can have me put in cage like a wild beast? So you and your medical experts can stand and watch me as you would a freak? You're a fool! You'll help me now! You'll do something—before it's too late! Do you hear me?"

The creature advanced slowly upon the doctor, and the girl backed away to the far wall, fear mirrored in her eyes.

Then Fred Trent stepped forward, his voice tense.

"Hold on, Gaddon—of course the doctor will help you—*won't* you, Fenwick?"

There was an urgent emphasis in Trent's last words, and his eyes caught those of the surgeon's, and held them in a meaningful look. He couldn't say what he wanted to, but the message in his eyes was imparted to Fenwick, and the doctor suddenly nodded.

"Yes—yes, of course ... But you'll have to remain quiet, Gaddon, and be patient a moment...."

The creature stopped its advance upon Fenwick then. And a growl rumbled in Gaddon's animal throat.

Then Fred watched as the doctor stepped swiftly to a table with instruments and hurriedly began to prepare a hypodermic.

"I'll give you a special extract injection to start...." Fenwick explained as he worked.

And Trent knew that the doctor was preparing an injection that would subdue the monster. That would enable them to call the police....

And the eyes of Gaddon watched the fingers of the surgeon prepare the hypodermic. And for a single moment the human part of Gaddon's monster mind relaxed its tenacious hold.

THERE was a rumble of raging thought deep within his twisted brain. It swept up, gripped the human element, and enveloped it. A hoarse mewing sound left the twisted lips as the mind became a single, bestial thing.

And now it thought with a viciousness. It knew now that it was finally in control. That the full change had been completed. And it knew suddenly what it wanted.

Its animal eyes stared at the three humans. And it felt a hatred for the men who did not understand it. And it felt a desire for the woman who feared it. A desire that crept out of the primeval jungles. That swept through it to find one of its kind. And there was the vague instinct that was Gaddon, who told it how to fulfill that desire. Gaddon, who knew where the secret lay.

And then there was the driving urge that swept up from the animal ages. The urge to kill, to destroy what was hated. And the eyes of the monster fastened on the figure of Fenwick as the doctor turned from the table, the hypodermic in his hand.

"All right, Gaddon ..."

The voice of Fenwick trailed off. And Fred Trent stared at the face of the monster. What he saw there brought a chill to his being. And he heard the girl gasp from the far corner of the room, as her eyes too saw the change that had spread over the face of the creature.

For there was no longer any vestige of human recognition in that face. There was no longer any trace of the man who had been Gaddon. There was only the monster now. The twisted, leering lips of an animal mind.

A harsh growl left those lips then and the creature moved forward toward the surgeon.

Trent knew what was happening, and he knew what he must do. There was death on that bestial face. Death that was reaching out ...

He heard the dim baying of the Great Dane from the rear of the house as he leaped forward.

Then his fist lashed out and caught the animal face in a lashing blow. His knuckles felt numb as he screamed:

"The hypodermic—doctor—quick!"

Then the creature turned on him and a long arm shot out. Trent felt a claw rake across his face and felt the burning bite of that claw sink into his flesh. Then, as he tried to dodge away from the beast and bring his fist up again, the monster leaped at him and Trent felt a powerful blow crash against his chin.

He spun back, falling to the floor, his head hitting the edge of an examining table. His senses reeled and he felt the blood running down his cheek, a warm, sticky stream that dripped to the floor.

He fought to keep his consciousness as he saw the beast turn away from him, satisfied that he was out of the way. Then he saw it leap at the stunned figure of Fenwick.

He heard the girl scream in terror and he saw Fenwick's arm come up with the hypodermic. He saw the doctor try to bring the needle down in a jab, but the monster's arm swept the needle aside and then a claw-like hand gripped Fenwick's throat.

There was a gasp of terror from Fenwick's lips as those fingers closed around his neck. Then the hypodermic fell from his nerveless hand and he fought to break away.

A deep rumbling growl spat from the lips of the monster as it closed with the struggling figure of Fenwick. Then the claws that were its hands raked the surgeon's throat in a feline rage.

Trent watched with numbed eyes, fighting back the wave of blackness that threatened to overcome him, and he saw the figure of Fenwick suddenly go limp in the grip of the monster.

He saw a spurt of blood burst from the man's torn throat, and then the creature dropped the limp body.

It fell to the floor, and a wave of red washed across the floor from the mangled throat. The monster stood over the lifeless body, a triumphant sound issuing from its twisted lips.

Then it turned toward the girl.

Trent tried to move. He tried to push back the weakness that numbed his body. But he couldn't. His head swam with the pain of the blow he had received, and he could only watch through half-closed eyes as the monster reached out for the girl.

Joan Drake screamed once as the long arms reached out for her. Then her voice ended abruptly as she fell to the floor in a faint.

The monster stood over her for a moment, then it reached down and picked up her body in its blood-splattered arms.

It turned for a moment, holding the girl, and shot a hate-filled glance at Trent's limp figure.

Then it moved swiftly across the room and out into the hall.

And the baying of the Great Dane sounded angrily in Fred Trent's ears ...

WITH a superhuman effort Fred Trent forced the numbness from his body and moved slowly to his feet. A horror gripped him that brought a new strength to his body, flooded it.

He stepped over the body of Fenwick, forcing his eyes away from the grisly sight of it as he dashed to the hallway.

"Joan—*Joan!*"

The girl's name came hoarsely from his lips as he ran into the hall and stared at the open door of the house. He ran to the door and out into the night.

His eyes stared wildly into the darkness, searching the street. But he saw nothing but his parked car at the curb. The monster had vanished. And with him, the unconscious girl.

A hopeless despair welled up inside Trent at that moment. For he knew he could never hope to find the creature now. And by the time help came it would be too late. They would find Joan's mangled body ...

The baying of the Great Dane rang in his ears then. The huge dog's howls of rage thundered in his ears and he heard the hound crash its great body against the closed door at the end of the hall, striving to get through.

And then a cry of hope left Trent's lips. He turned and ran back into the house. He grabbed the long leash from its wall hook beside the rear door and then he swung the door partway open.

"Brutus! Quiet, Brutus!"

The head of the Great Dane struggled through the partly opened door, a snarl of rage welling from the huge dog's mouth as Trent shouted at it.

Then he slipped the leash into its metal ring around the neck of the dog and pulled the door open.

The animal rushed into the hall, nearly tearing the leash from Fred Trent's hands as it lunged forward.

The dog paused beside the open door of the consultation room where the body of Fenwick lay dead and still on the floor. The animal lifted its muzzle and sniffed the air. A howl of anguished rage left it then and Trent knew that the dog sensed its master had been murdered. And then it caught the scent of the monster, the thing that had caused its wild rage to be unleashed, and it leaped forward, down the hall and out the front door into the night.

Trent held the leash tightly in his hands, running behind the straining dog, jumping over a low hedge after the animal as it headed down the shadowed street to the edge of the city.

And then the last house was behind them and Trent was racing behind the dog out into the desert land beyond.

HIS breath was an aching fire in his throat. His legs were numbed beyond feeling. They were parts of his body that simply refused to stop moving, though every nerve and muscle in them screamed in protest.

It seemed like he had been running for hours, half tripping, stumbling across the darkened ground behind the seemingly tireless body of the Great Dane.

They ran in near silence now. Only the sounds of their labored breathing mingled with the night wind. The howls of rage no longer issued from the throat of the huge dog. There was only its panting breath, and the strain of its mighty body as it sought to tear loose from the man holding it.

But Trent held grimly to the leash, running as fast as his numbed body would go.

And he knew he could not go much further. That soon he would drop to the ground in exhaustion. That his last reserve of energy was nearly spent.

And then his eyes peered through the darkness ahead and he saw a glow of lights in the distance. And suddenly he knew those lights. And he became aware of where they were racing toward.

It was the Rocket Proving Grounds!

And the fence of the government project loomed close ahead.

And as they neared the fence, Trent's eyes pierced the darkness and he saw a jagged tear in the metal mesh of the fence. A tear that stood as high as a man, a hole through which a man could have entered.

The Great Dane bounded toward that hole and Trent followed the dog through it. He felt the animal pause momentarily and he nearly stumbled over a body lying on the ground at his feet just inside the fence.

His heart stood still for a moment and the girl's name sped to his lips. But he never uttered the word. For he suddenly saw that it was the body of a guard. A body whose torn throat lay red and gory in death.

And then the Great Dane let a howl of anger out on the night wind, and the beast leaped forward again, Trent running behind it.

And ahead of them, Trent saw a great looming shape in the darkness, and as his eyes fell upon it, a despairing terror gripped him.

It was the second rocket! Standing in its cradle, silent in the night, a shaft of metal that looked skyward.

And a realization of what the monster had in mind struck him. He knew now where they were headed. He knew why the monster had torn the fence, why a guard had been killed where he stood.

And as if the thought had been a prelude, he saw the rocket loom before them as the Great Dane bounded around its base.

And he saw the metal stairway leading up to the middle of the giant projectile.

And at the top of those stairs, going into the now open rocket chamber, was the monster, holding the unconscious girl in its arms.

The Great Dane saw the creature in the same instant. And a terrible howl of rage welled from its throat. It gave a lunge forward then that broke Trent's grip from the leash he held. And the dog was free.

THE monster turned in the same moment and saw them. A roar of feline anger left its throat as the huge dog leaped up the steps toward the platform above.

The monster dropped the girl's body on the narrow platform and backed toward the opening of the rocket chamber.

Then the Great Dane reached the platform and poised itself for a leap.

Trent was dashing forward toward the stairs as the dog's body flew through the air. He saw the flashing jaws of the animal snap at the throat of the monster, as its heavy body smashed against it.

Then the arms of the creature were tearing at the dog as it was forced back into the rocket chamber.

Trent's feet flew up the stairs, his breath a tortured gasp in his throat. He saw the girl stir on the platform, as consciousness returned to her.

"Joan!"

Her name sped from his lips as he reached the top step. Then his hands closed around the girl's shoulders, lifting her to her feet.

The snarl of the Great Dane reached his ears from the rocket chamber, and the answering roar of rage from the monster as they fought. His eyes saw the vague, terrible shadows of them, heard the snapping jaws of the dog, and the raking claws.

And then he was dragging the girl down the steps.

They reached the ground and Trent pulled her away from the rocket, felt her come to life in his arms, heard the sob on her lips.

But his head turned away from her and he stared anxiously up at the open rocket chamber.

He heard the bodies of the monster and the dog slam against the inner side of the chamber, and then he saw the door of the rocket close. He knew that the automatic mechanism must have been touched in the battle.

And even as the thought ran through his mind he heard a sudden roar of flaming sound. The night lit up in a sheet of brilliant light and a wave of flame spread out from the base of the rocket.

Trent pulled the girl away from that blinding sheet of exploding energy, and his eyes stared in grim fascination as they ran.

He saw the rocket shudder in its cradle and then lift slowly. It was as if time had turned back and he were watching an identical scene that had happened earlier that day.

Only it wasn't the same scene. It was now a scene of horror. For he knew that the monster and the dog were in that rocket. The rocket that would shoot skyward in moments, even as its companion had done. Would reach into the outer fringes of the Earth's atmosphere where the cosmic rays would envelop it, would react upon the animals inside it.

And a terrible dread spread through Trent at the thought. For if the first change had been terrible enough, what would happen now?

And as he thought, he saw the rocket lift slowly from its cradle and gather speed as it shot upward into the night.

THE blinding light of the exploding rocket fuel lit the proving grounds like a huge beacon of incandescence, and Trent was aware of shouts ahead of him, and running feet.

Then he was surrounded by men from the project, and he caught the glint of alert weapons and uniforms.

He felt arms grab him and the girl and heard questions pounding at him.

But then he saw a face he knew. And he tore away from the arms of the guards and shouted.

"Dr. Mathieson! Listen to me!"

The scientist stepped up to him and Trent gripped his arm in the fading light of the vanishing rocket.

"What's happened here?" the scientist demanded. "Aren't you one of the newsmen—"

Trent interrupted him. He poured out a string of words. Words that told what had happened. And as he talked he saw the eyes of the scientist widen in disbelief. And he heard the guards grow silent around him. Felt every ear listening with awe to his words.

And when he had finished there was a long moment of silence. And then Joan Drake moved tremblingly up beside Trent and she spoke:

"It's true, doctor! Every word Fred said is true!"

And one of the guards broke in:

"The word just came in from post four. The fence was torn to pieces—and Giddings has been murdered—just as they said!"

Then the silence again. And the face of Mathieson was grim as Trent broke through the quiet:

"—Doctor—that monster who was Gaddon—he's up there now! When the cosmic rays change him and the dog and the chamber is released ..."

The scientist shook his head slowly, a look of awe in his eyes.

"It won't release, Trent," he said.

Fred Trent looked at him questioningly.

"Gaddon must have forgotten one thing," the scientist continued. "That rocket was also an experimental project. But not for the same purpose. It was to test a new type of explosive ..."

Mathieson's voice trailed off and silence closed over the small group then.

There was no need to say anything further. There was only the tension of waiting, the tension that showed in every eye.

And the girl moved closer to Trent, her body trembling against his.

They waited. The seconds passed like moments in eternity. Slowly they marched by, one by one. And then a minute. And the tension grew.

They heard it then. Off in the distance. Out in the waste of the open desert land. A thundering sound. An explosion that rolled in a wave of sound.

And with it a flash of brilliant light. Light that seared through the night in a terrible wave. And with it the thunder of the explosive warhead.

And then silence.

After a long moment the voice of Mathieson came through the quiet night wind.

"... It's over. Gaddon is—dead. Poor fool, he fumbled with the tools of creation, tools that man is not ready to wield ..."

And Trent heard one of the soldiers gasp, "What a story! *What* a story!"

But he knew, as he held the girl against him, felt her body relax beside his, that it was a story he didn't want to write.

He wanted only to forget ...